Gallop-o-gallop

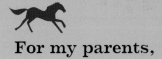

For my parents,

who listened to my horse dreams and made them come true—S.A.

To my brother Josie,

for countless hours of watching me ride in circles—K.M.

DIAL BOOKS FOR YOUNG READERS
A division of Penguin Young Readers Group
Published by The Penguin Group
Penguin Group (USA) Inc., 375 Hudson Street, New York, NY 10014, U.S.A.
Penguin Group (Canada), 90 Eglinton Avenue East, Suite 700, Toronto, Ontario, Canada M4P 2Y3 (a division of Pearson Penguin Canada Inc.)
Penguin Books Ltd, 80 Strand, London WC2R 0RL, England
Penguin Ireland, 25 St. Stephen's Green, Dublin 2, Ireland (a division of Penguin Books Ltd)
Penguin Group (Australia), 250 Camberwell Road, Camberwell, Victoria 3124, Australia (a division of Pearson Australia Group Pty Ltd)
Penguin Books India Pvt Ltd, 11 Community Centre, Panchsheel Park, New Delhi - 110 017, India
Penguin Group (NZ), Cnr Airborne and Rosedale Roads, Albany, Auckland 1310, New Zealand (a division of Pearson New Zealand Ltd)
Penguin Books (South Africa) (Pty) Ltd, 24 Sturdee Avenue, Rosebank, Johannesburg 2196, South Africa
Penguin Books Ltd, Registered Offices: 80 Strand, London WC2R 0RL, England

Designed by Teresa Kietlinski Dikun
Text set in Barbera
Manufactured in China on acid-free paper
10 9 8 7 6 5 4 3 2 1
LIBRARY OF CONGRESS CATALOGING-IN-PUBLICATION DATA
Alonzo, Sandra.
Gallop-o-gallop / by Sandra Alonzo ; pictures by Kelly Murphy.
p.   cm.
ISBN 978-0-8037-2967-4
1. Horses—Juvenile poetry. 2. Horsemanship—Juvenile poetry. 3. Children's poetry, American. I. Murphy, Kelly, date. II. Title.
PS3601.L63G35 2007   811'.6—dc22   2005012068

The art was done with watercolor, acrylic, and gel medium on paper.

GALLOP O GALLOP

by
Sandra Alonzo

pictures by

Kelly Murphy

Dial Books for Young Readers

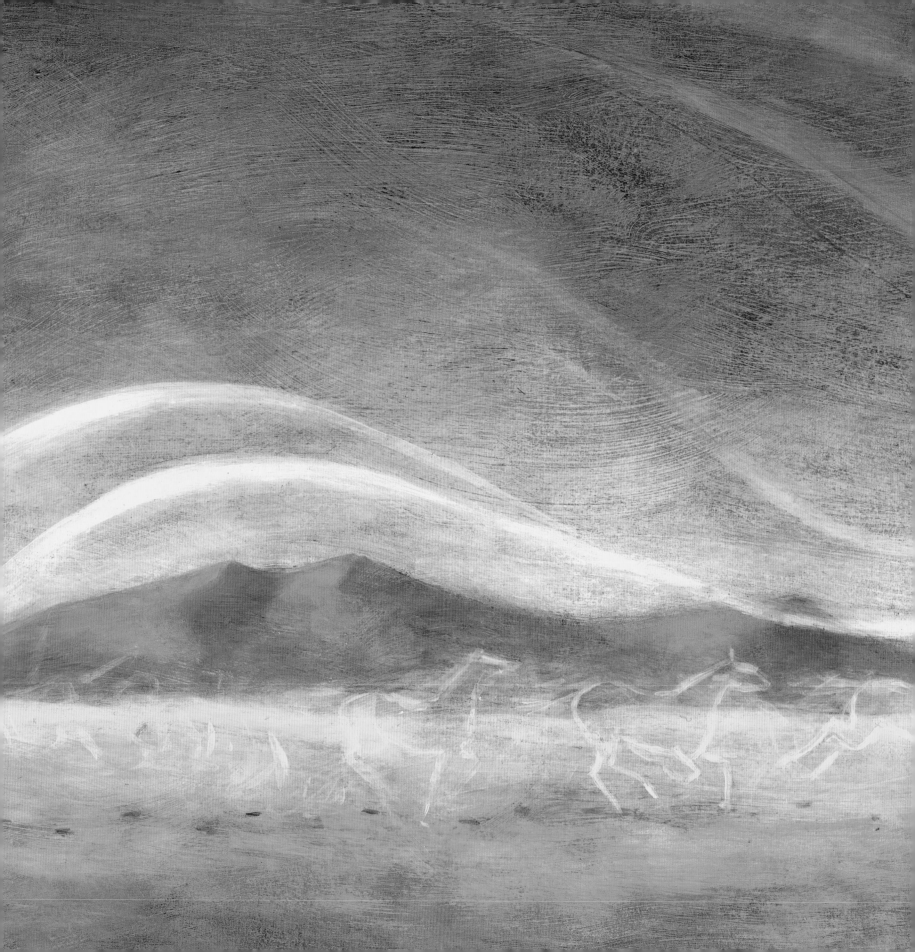

Gallop-o-Gallop

Gallop-o-gallop-o-gallop along
Singing-o-singing-o-singing a song.
Swift over hills, carry me there
    The wind on my face
      the sky in my hair.
Gallop-o-gallop-o-gallop so fast
A trail so long, a journey so vast.
We travel as one, bound to the end
    My horse is my heart
      my horse is my friend.

The Birth

"Wake up! Wake up! It's almost time!"
Mom's voice crept in where I'd slept warm.
I pulled on boots and heavy coat,
Then marched in darkness through the storm.

The barn was cold but it was dry;
The wind slammed hard against the door.
There Peaches pawed in knee-deep straw,
Then paced and paced the earthen floor.

Next, Peaches lay on bulging sides
And moaned, but didn't move about.
I worried as the minutes passed
Until Mom gasped, "Front hooves are out!"

Then Mom knelt down in fragrant straw;
"Your mare is doing fine," she said.
As rain struck fiercely on the roof,
I knelt down too, and saw the head.

I reached for Mom and held her hand,
And soon the baby, wet and whole,
Came sliding forth as Peaches turned
To whinny at her brand-new foal.

I think I cried . . . I know I laughed.
The storm had cleared by early morn.
I do know something changed in me,
That wondrous night our foal was born.

My Little One

You're safe, my dear, my little one,
You know that I'm your ma.
It's time . . . it's time
To struggle up;
I'll keep you close to me.

It's work, I know, my tiny foal,
You're thrashing, wrestling hard.
It's time . . . it's time
To strain and stand;
You have so much to see.

You're up, you're up,
   my brave new babe,
And nursing by my side.
It's time . . . it's time
For wobbly steps,
And soon you'll
      gallop free.

Greeting

Shoulders shudder
Nostrils quiver
Ears to tail
Whole Horse Shiver

Neeeeeigh!

Color Scheme

Applaud the silver Lipizzans
And gasp at Palomino gold,
While Buckskins strut their tans and black,
Those Pinto patches stand out bold.

An Appaloosa shows off spots;
Icelandics come in every hue.
Distinctive Tarpan's legs are striped;
Albino white shines pure and true.

Compared with such flamboyancy,
My pony's lovely coat is plain.
Yet when he rolls in grassy fields,
He flaunts a MOST amazing stain!

Appaloosa, Rappaloosa

App-app
Rap-rap
Give a little clap-clap.

Flap-flap
Snap-snap
Tell your toes to tap-tap.

Spot-spot
Trot-trot
NOW you're gettin' hot-hot!

Appa-loosa
Appa-loosa
Rap around a Rappaloosa!

Horse Grooming

Grooming kit
Dusting mitt
Gel and goo
Blue shampoo.

Braids and bows
"Horsie" clothes
Insect sprays
Wax and glaze.

Brushes, combs
Scented foams.
Lookin' fine
My CLEAN equine!

But he can't wait
        To pass our gate
                And sweetly stroll,
                        quickly drop . . .
                                and roll . . .
                                        and roll . . .

Horse Talk

I'm just a horse; I cannot talk,
And that's a critter's fate.
But if you heed my actions, folks,
We might communicate!

You wonder why I toss my head?
My teeth bang on that bit!
The reason why I sometimes buck?
My saddle doesn't fit!

You think I'm being picky when
I won't eat hay that's bad.
And when you pull my cinch too tight?
You don't know why I'm mad!

I'm pastured with a horse that kicks,
And that's why I look grim.
You say I'm clumsy when I trip,
But horse hooves need a trim!

I'm really not a crazy mount.
I have no stubborn streak.
But since I can't say human words,
My actions have to speak!

The Sneeze

A horse's sneeze erupts
With unexpected power.
Duck or run for cover or
Prepare to take a shower!

Wild One

When I peer through the fence
Her muscles twitch.
She's scrawny,
Caked with mud,
Proud and scared . . .
. . . and she's mine.
Carefully, slowly,
I sneak my hand
Through weathered boards.
The wild one snorts, spins around, and
Bolts to the far edge of the pen.
"It's okay, girl," I whisper.
"One day you'll be my friend."

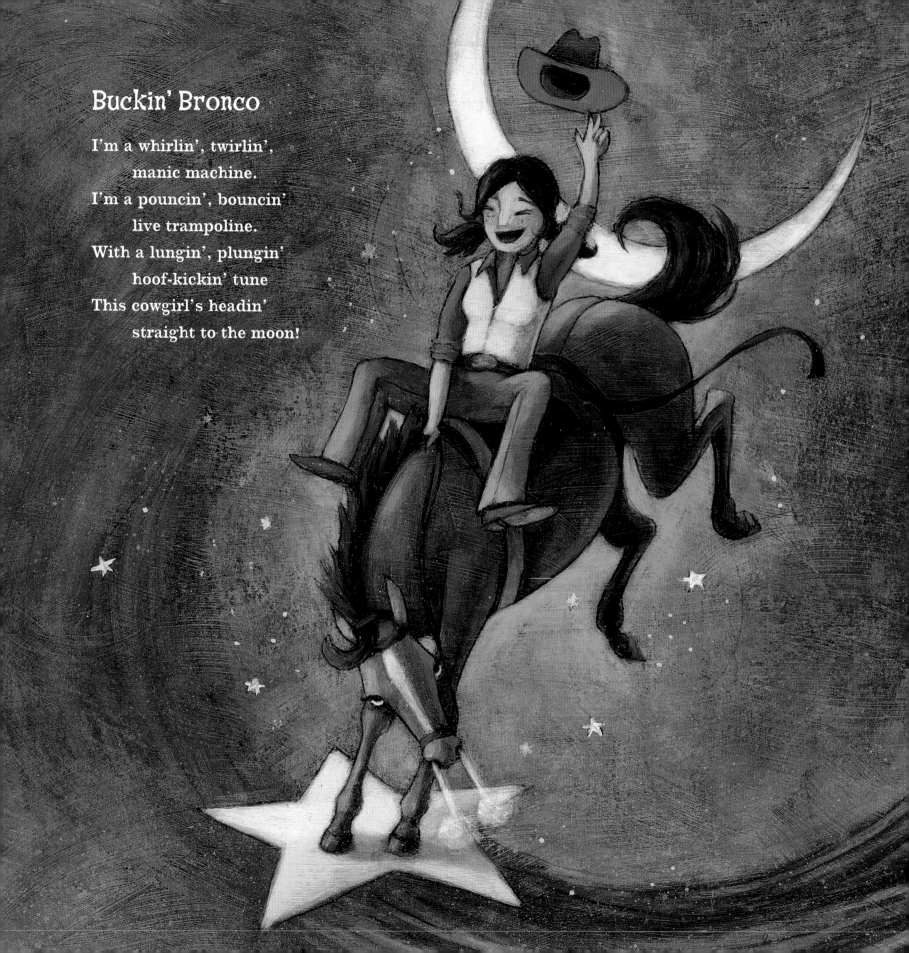

Buckin' Bronco

I'm a whirlin', twirlin',
   manic machine.
I'm a pouncin', bouncin'
   live trampoline.
With a lungin', plungin'
   hoof-kickin' tune
This cowgirl's headin'
   straight to the moon!

Sea Horse

My sea horse can
    swish
        with
            fish
Near lacy seaweed.

My sea horse can
    splash
        and
            crash
Through MONSTER waves!

Oh, how we
    prance
        and
            dance
As the swells advance,
Then back to the shore
We CHARGE!

Stampede!

Like a storm cloud spewing dust
An earthquake of hooves thunders by
Rumbling, rumbling
Growling deep in the prairie's belly
Vibrating the earth
Echoing, echoing
Sweeping wide over grassy plains
Vanishing into ancient hills
Fading to a quiet hummmmmmm . . .
    . . . and now . . .
        . . . all is still.

The Track

I sit in the stands when we're at the track
And root for the horse who lags at the back.
My shouts float away to that horse in the rear,
Who might hear my yell and then shift a gear.

Will he gallop up front to finish the race?
Will we hear them announce his name in first place?
There's one thing I've learned when underdogs win:
It's where you end up, NOT where you begin!

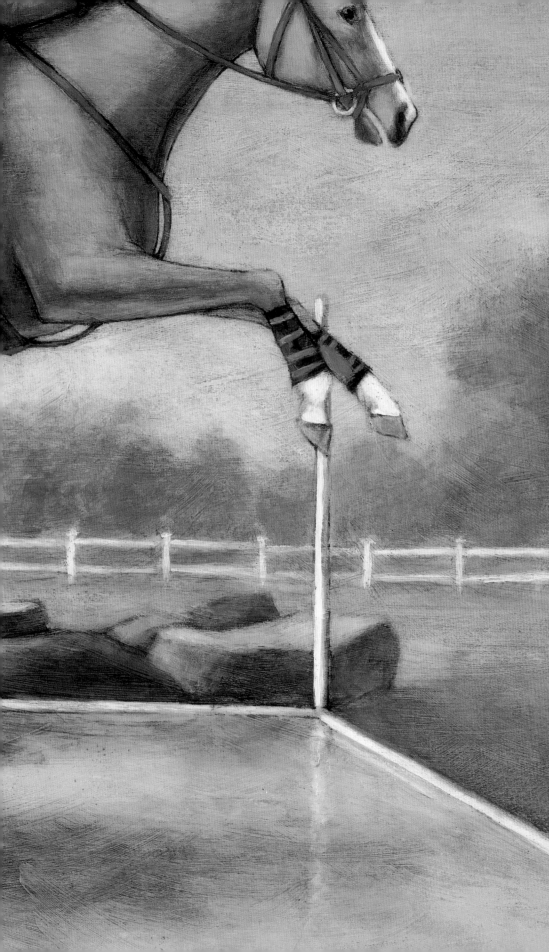

Jumping Competition

My jumper cruises
To the water hurdle,
Leaps mud and rails.
We fly with such grace,
The crowd gasps as he sails—
The rails stay up!

My jumper soars,
Airborne with joy,
Ears alert, belly heaving,
He clears each obstacle.
The crowd stops breathing—
The rails stay up!

My jumper gallops,
Double jump is next.
He circles round to glide,
Hits ground and springs again.
The crowd sighs with each stride—
The rails stay up!

My jumper prances.
Winners' names are called.
I stroke his neck with my hands,
The blue ribbon is ours.
The crowd cheers in the stands!
ALL RAILS STAYED UP!

Winter Horse

Shaggy
Furry
Rugged
Puffy mop of hair.
Is it really you
Hiding under there?

Old Horse

Old horse
Lumbers, lumbers
To the fence.
With noisy, flapping lips,
He fumbles for carrots
From my waiting,
Outstretched hand.
I pat his whiskered nose.
Do you remember,
Old horse,
Those grand parades and fancy shows
They say you entered years ago?
I hear you were the best, old horse,
So you deserve this rest.
Yes,
You deserve this rest.

Sleigh Ride

Our driver has a long white beard;
A Santa Claus without the suit.
We hop into his warm red sleigh;
He calls out, "Yah!" and stamps his boot.

With jing-jing-jingly bouncy tunes
Four flying hooves pull out with ease.
Our cheeks turn pink in icy air,
The reins slap-slapping through the trees.

We slip by farms in sleeping snow
As flurries capture woodsy smells,
Our sleigh skim-skimming smooth and swift,
We softly sway to singing bells.

Night Ride

Warily we wind down paths
Where ghostly creatures lurk.
The empty air
Grabs eerie sounds:
    coyote's howl
        bobcat's growl
           stray dog's yowl
Even though I tremble on his back,
My mount is steady, calm, and true.
With careful steps
He guides us into
Shivering, shifting shadows.

At last a light
Shines far ahead through
Strong, familiar trees.
My knees relax,
My breathing calms,
We're home, we're home, we're home!

Bedtime Book

A shimmering, glimmering,
Silvery form
Escapes in a swirl
From a page that's torn.
He circles my room
With his magical horn.
Through the window he zooms!
Come back, unicorn!

The Trail

How many times
Have we followed this trail
And each time found
Something new?

Sage, like perfumed velvet,
Brushes against
My jeans, my boots.
Wings *whirrrrrr* as
Quail burst from quiet bushes,
Startling my horse and me.

We follow the trail
Cautiously stepping over rocks,
Splashing into the creek.
SSSSSS—a snake *ssssssslides*
Under cattails that sway,
Keeping time
As we shimmy on through.

Muscles strain
As I lean forward in the saddle.
We're climbing, climbing.
High up, the meadow sings with insects;
Flowers sparkle like stars
In a grassy green sky.

We follow the trail
Traveling deep into the
     tree
     tunnel
     where it's cool,
     damp,
     dim,
     and smells like mushrooms.

Skirting past the gigantic oak,
My horse spooks.
A bouncing cotton ball
Dives into the chaparral.
A rabbit!
I squeeze gently with my knees
And we continue on.

I feel our quickening pace,
See the stable beckoning,
Know my horse's urgency.

But, oh, how I wish
we could
follow
the
trail
forever.